The FEEL GOOD Book

TODD PARR

Megan Tingley Books

LITTLE, BROWN AND COMPANY

New York   Boston

This book is
dedicated to everyone.
FEEL GOOD!

Especially to all those who have made me feel good:
Bully, Tammy, Jerry, Dad, Candy, Grandma, Liz, Gerry,
Dawn, Sandy, Sara, Bill, Karen, Greg, and Jane.

I love you,
Todd

Little, Brown and Company

Hachette Book Group
237 Park Avenue, New York, NY 10017
Visit our website at www.lb-kids.com

Little, Brown and Company is a division of Hachette Book Group, Inc.
The Little, Brown name and logo are trademarks of Hachette Book Group, Inc.

First Paperback Edition: April 2009
Originally published in hardcover in September 2002 by Little, Brown and Company

Library of Congress Cataloging-in-Publication Data

Parr, Todd.
   The feel good book / Todd Parr.—1st ed.
      p.   cm.
"Megan Tingley Books."
Summary: Relates things that make people feel good.
[1. Happiness—Fiction.] I. Title
PZ7.P2447 Fdg 2002
[E]—dc21   2001050478
ISBN 978-0-316-04345-8 (PB) / ISBN 978-0-316-07206-9 (HC 10x10) / ISBN 978-0-316-15565-6 (HC 9x9)

10 9 8 7 6 5 4 3

IM

Printed in China

Giving a great, big hug feels good

Eating carrots with a bunny feels good

Getting tickled
feels good

Taking a bubble bath feels good

Showing the new kid around feels good

Rubbing noses feels good

Visiting a sick friend feels good

Crying when you're sad feels good

Laughing out loud feels good

Brushing your hair
with a lion feels good

Catching snowflakes on your tongue feels good

Watching your grandma
and grandpa dance
feels good

Having a ladybug land on your hand feels good

Sharing your treats
feels good

Waiting for the tooth fairy feels good

Saying "I love you" in sign language feels good.

Playing under the sprinkler feels good

Making a new friend feels good

Making sounds like a monkey feels good

Seeing fireflies outside your window feels good

Dog

Letting a kitten lick your fingers feels good

Brushing your teeth with strawberry toothpaste feels good

Learning how to count to 8 with a spider feels good

Being brave feels good

Taking a nap with a giant stuffed animal feels good

Being together feels good

It FEELS GOOD to think about all the things that make you FEEL GOOD. Rubbing my dog's tummy makes me FEEL GOOD— and him, too. What things make you FEEL GOOD?

LOVE,
Todd